For Dan: my husband and best friend. Thank you for your laughter, your encouragement, and for being my voice of reason.

Cindy McKinley

For the peacemakers.

Mary Gregg Byrne

ILLUMINATION
Arts

PUBLISHING COMPANY, L.L.C.
P. O. Box 1865, Bellevue, WA 98009
Tel: 425-968-5097 ∗ Fax: 425-968-5634
lifeinfo@illumin.com ∗ www.illumin.com

Library of Congress Cataloging-in-Publication Data

McKinley, Cindy, 1968-

One Voice/written by Cindy McKinley; illustrated by Mary Gregg Byrne.
p. cm.

Summary: One boy's act of kindness sparks a wave of goodwill that circles through his community and eventually comes around back to him.
ISBN 978-0-9855417-0-5

[1. Voice—Fiction. 2. Kindness—Fiction.] I. Byrne, Mary Gregg, 1951-, ill. II. Title.

PZ7.M19867 On 2013
[E]—dc21   2013024506

Publisher's Appreciation:

A heartfelt thanks to our outstanding editing team—Ruth Thompson, Kelley Frodel, Siri Alderson, Stuart Moore, Megan Hyde, Alexandra Bell, Haley Larson, Sara Bjelke, Jacquelyn Grambush, Julie Ropelewski, Ian Wyant, Cristina Ralston, Tara O'Berry, Amanda Weiland, Ashley Goodwin, Alexandra Hughes-Wooton, Christine Texeira, Jenn Sundt, Arlena Pickrel, and Maggie Karl. Special thanks to our brilliant designer, Lana Carolan, whose creative touch has helped greatly in the birth of this beautiful treasure.

INSPIRE EVERY CHILD FOUNDATION

A portion of the profits from this book will be donated to Inspire Every Child, a non-profit foundation dedicated to helping disadvantaged children around the world. This organization provides inspirational children's books to individuals and groups that are directly involved in supporting the welfare of children. Your help in supporting this crucial cause would be greatly appreciated. For more information, please visit www.inspire-every-child.org.

First Printing 2013
Published in the United States of America
Printed in China by Chenxi International Industrial, Ltd.
Book Designer: Lana Carolan

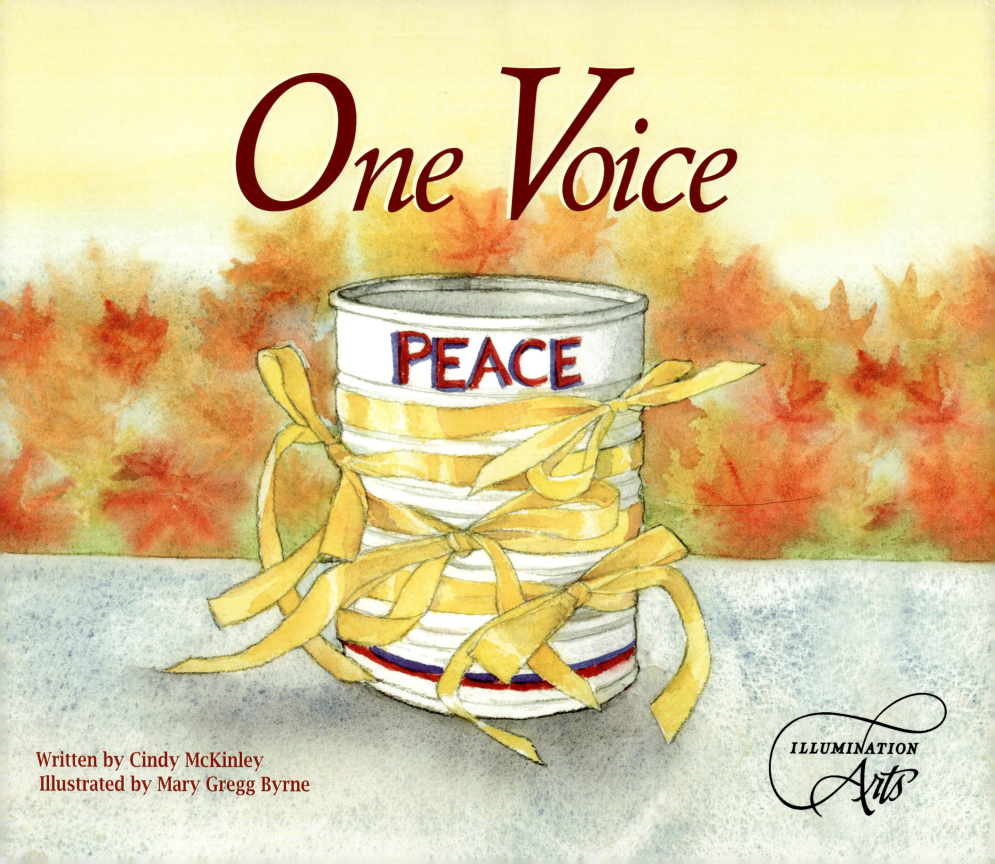

One Voice

PEACE

Written by Cindy McKinley
Illustrated by Mary Gregg Byrne

ILLUMINATION Arts

"Today's the day!" Jacob whispered to himself. While standing at the bus stop, he thought of all the places a boy could go to ask for donations. He couldn't wait to start working on his new project. When the bus arrived, it was more crowded than usual, and Jacob sat in the last empty seat.

At the next stop, a woman stepped onto the bus. Jacob noticed that she would soon be having a baby, so he stood up politely and said, "Here, you can take my seat."

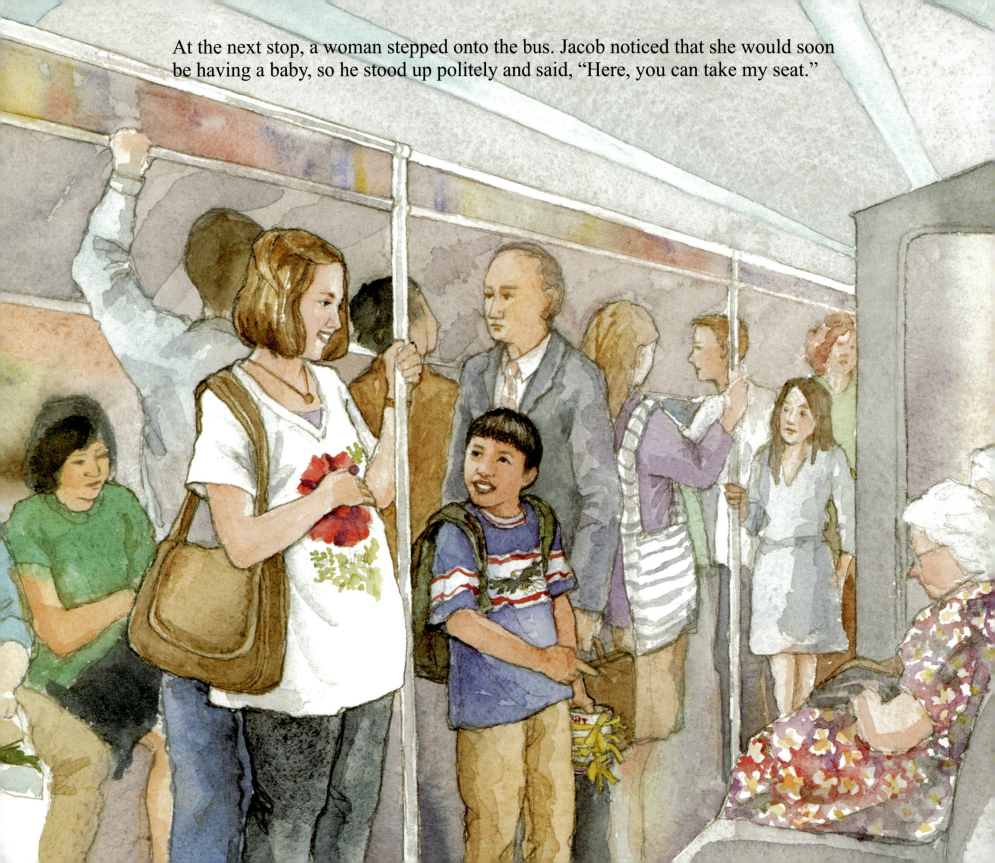

The woman was touched by the boy's thoughtful gesture and asked about his colorful donation can wrapped in bright yellow ribbons. As Jacob excitedly explained his project, she dropped a few shiny coins that jingled into the empty can. "Good luck with your project," she said. "The world needs more people like you."

While walking home from the bus stop, the woman noticed that her neighbor's recycling bin was still sitting by the road. Even though she'd had a tiring day, she thought about the young boy on the bus and was inspired to pass on his kindness.

She started pulling the bin up the driveway, then paused to chat with the mailman. He was sorry to hear that her elderly neighbor had not been feeling well.

Mrs. Johnson was on her front porch enjoying the beautiful day when she saw two people walking up the driveway. Her thoughtful neighbor was bringing her recycling bin back from the curb, and the mailman was bringing the mail right up to her house!

"Thank you so much," she said warmly. "I really appreciate your help." She clipped a few daisies from her flower planter and gave them each a small bouquet.

The mailman could imagine how difficult it must be for Mrs. Johnson to walk down her long driveway, so he decided to bring the mail to her door every day. He carefully tucked the daisies into his shirt pocket and began whistling a happy tune as he continued along his route.

At another house, the mailman noticed a young girl sitting alone on her porch with a skateboard. He remembered that her family was new to the neighborhood, so he took a daisy from his pocket and handed it to her with a friendly smile. "You know," he said, "there's a park nearby with a great place for skateboarding."

The girl had been missing her friends and her old neighborhood, so the mailman's suggestion really cheered her up. She found the park and had lots of fun skating all afternoon, but she was sad to see so much trash littering the ground.

Grateful to have a new place to skate, the girl
decided to return the next day to clean up the park.

The next morning, a boy was in the park playing basketball with his friends when he noticed a girl picking up trash near the court.

Suddenly inspired to help, he finished his game early and joined her.
By working together, they were able to clean up the entire park.

On his way home, the boy noticed a sign requesting donations of children's books for a local charity's fundraiser.

Still feeling inspired by the girl's example, he decided to go around his neighborhood collecting books to help the children.

At the fundraising event, a dentist purchased some children's books for the waiting room in his office. A few weeks later, a little boy arrived early for his appointment and picked up one of the donated books. The cheerful story brought a smile to his face. He usually felt nervous about going to the dentist, but after reading this book, he was able to relax.

When the appointment was over, the boy chose a pencil from the prize box that said, "You Are Special." But instead of keeping it, he gave the pencil to the dentist. "This is for you," he said. "Thanks for being so nice and for doing such a great job on my teeth!"

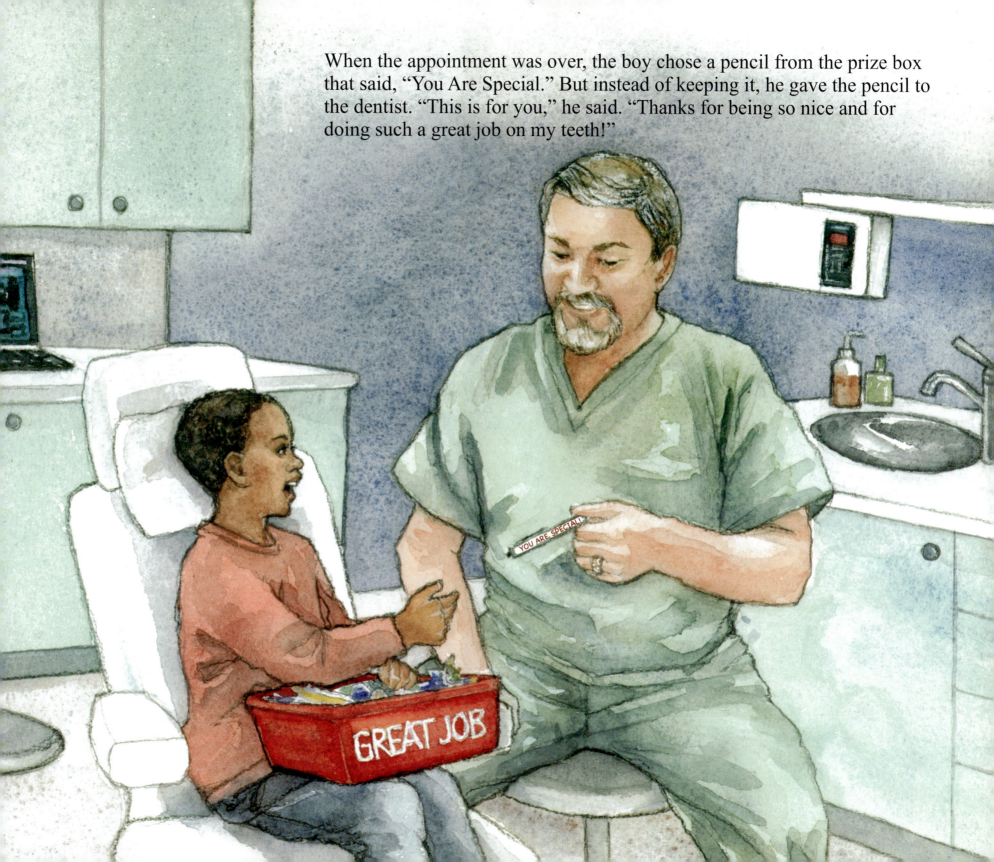

At dinner that evening, the dentist told his family about the boy's gift and how much it had brightened his day. The story made his daughter happy because she knew that few people thought about thanking her dad for taking care of their teeth.

Wanting to share her happiness, the girl ran up to her room after dinner and made a special card with brightly colored ribbons. It was for her teacher, who would be visiting her class the next day after being away for a while.

The next day, the girl went to school early. She couldn't wait to see her teacher, who was bringing her newborn son.

All the kids were excited to meet the baby, and the teacher loved seeing her students again. After opening the pretty card, she gave the girl a big "thank you" hug and promised her class that she would be returning soon.

On her way home, the teacher stopped by the park,
where a special ceremony was being held to
celebrate the town's new Peace Pole Memorial.

As she walked closer to the stage, she was surprised to see a young boy standing at the microphone. After a moment, she recognized him—it was the boy who had given her his seat on the bus!

Jacob thanked everyone for helping him raise enough money to buy the four young maple trees planted around the new Peace Pole. "I hope this memorial will inspire everyone," he said.

"If we all work together, we can make the world a more beautiful and peaceful place. I believe that each one of us, no matter how big or small, can make a difference in this world. All we have to do is try."

The ceremony ended and everyone cheered. After waving to his proud mom, Jacob took the yellow ribbons from his collection can and began tying one around each tree. But when he reached the fourth tree, he realized that the last ribbon was missing!

Seeing the disappointed look on Jacob's face, the teacher stepped forward to offer him the yellow ribbon from her card. He was so surprised he didn't know what to say. This was the same woman he had met on the bus several weeks earlier.

But now she was holding her new baby. Not only that, she was also holding just the ribbon he needed! "Thank you so much," Jacob said as he tied the new ribbon around the last tree. "I wish my dad could be here to see this. He's away on duty, and I really miss him."

Jacob's wish brought a tear to the teacher's eye. "What you said up there was really inspiring, and I'll bet your dad is very proud of you. You've shown that everyone can make a difference and, most of all..."

"...that even one small voice can change the world."

Curriculum Connections Page
For Teachers, Parents, and Kids

Questions to Discuss with Your Family

1. What can you do to brighten someone's day?
2. What can you avoid doing that would make someone's life more peaceful?
3. How can you use your time to help make your home, school, or community a better place?
4. How can you use your words to make the world a better place?
5. What does peace mean to you?
6. Is there a Peace Pole near your school or community? What does it symbolize to you?

You Can Make a Difference!
Here Are Some Ways You Can Get Involved in Your Community:

Planting Trees: There are many benefits from planting trees:
* Trees improve the quality of our air and water.
* Trees absorb carbon dioxide and release the oxygen we need in order to breathe.
* Trees provide habitat, food, and protection for many animals.
* Trees make our world a more beautiful place.

Peace Poles: Peace Poles present the message and prayer "May Peace Prevail on Earth" in a wide array of languages, symbolizing the oneness of humanity and our common wish for a peaceful world. There are many thousands of Peace Poles, and they can be seen on every continent, even Antarctica! When you raise one in your community, you are connecting with countless people who all share the same wish.

Book Drives: Book drives are a wonderful way your school or group can help your entire community. Reading skills are important both in and out of the classroom. The more students read for fun, the better readers they become, helping them to succeed in school and in life. Putting books into children's hands can change not only their lives but their families and the community as a whole. Running your own book drive can be a really fun and satisfying experience. But it can also take a lot of work, such as making plans, creating posters, and arranging drop-off boxes. To be safe, younger children should always ask a grown-up to help with collections.

Here's a Challenge!

Try to say or do at least one kind thing every day. Before going to sleep, review the good deeds you did that day that made you feel proud. Take time to think about the kind things other people did that helped make your day brighter. Remember: Even if you help just one person feel happier, you have changed the world.

"Tie a Yellow Ribbon Round the Old Oak Tree" is a well-loved song in America. For many people, yellow ribbons remind them of loved ones who are absent and will be warmly welcomed upon their return home. Especially during times of war, they are used to show people's support for our troops.

More inspiring picture books from Illumination Arts

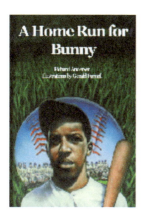

A Home Run For Bunny
Richard Andersen/Gerald Purnell
ISBN 978-0-9855417-2-9

When racial prejudice keeps one player off the field, the team must make a difficult choice—to stay and play for the championship, or to stand up for the rights of their teammate.

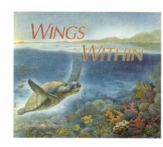

Wings Within
Franklin Hill/Aries Cheung
ISBN 978-0-615-50779-8

In this compelling sequel to *Wings of Change*, Myrtle the sea turtle is determined to grow wings like her butterfly friend, Anew.

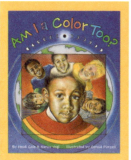

Am I a Color Too?
Heidi Cole & Nancy Vogl/Gerald Purnell
ISBN 978-0-9740190-5-5

A bi-racial boy wonders why people are identified by the color of their skin rather than by what really matters.

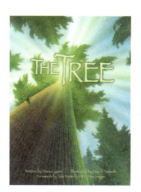

The Tree
Dana Lyons/David Danioth
ISBN 978-0-9701907-1-0

The poignant song of an 800-year-old Douglas fir entreats us to protect our fragile environment.

One Smile
Cindy McKinley/Mary Gregg Byrne
ISBN 978-0-935699-23-4

A young girl's innocent smile sparks a chain reaction of kindness and goodwill that touches her entire community before finally coming full circle to bless her and her family.

Just Imagine
John Thompson & George Schultz/Wodin
ISBN 978-0-9740190-6-2

Children let their imaginations run wild as they work and play, always protected by loving hands.

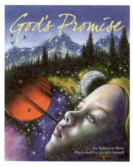

God's Promise
Maureen Moss/Gerald Purnell
ISBN 978-0-9740190-7-9

Before her birth, God helps Angelina prepare for her wondrous new life on Earth.

We Share One World
Jane E. Hoffelt/Marty Husted
ISBN 978-0-9701907-8-9

Children around the world discover how sharing the same planet connects us directly with people from all lands and backgrounds.

You can view the entire Illumination Arts collection at www.illumin.com.